Midway Library

W9-ANX-569

There is nothing too good to be true

Ram Dass

THE ROCKING HORSE ANGEL

Story and Pictures by Mercer Mayer

MARSHALL CAVENDISH   NEW YORK

"Oh he'll just love it, dear," said the woman as she and her husband gazed at the rocking horse in the window.

"Why, yes he will," said the man as they went inside. "How much?" he asked the shopkeeper. They agreed on a price, and the little dappled-gray rocking horse was lifted up from her place of so many years.

The man carried her outside and put her in the back of an old black pickup truck. Off they went, bumpity, bump, through the countryside to a farm, a boy, and an adventure that was waiting.

The rocking horse didn't know it, but she was to be a Christmas present for a boy. A boy who loved horses, a boy who loved to play and dream. A boy who would need her help.

The days of summer came to an end and great cloud giants from the north began their journey high over the farm. The blue of the heavens took on a deeper hue, letting everyone know that the hazy heat of summer was past. When summer fades, boys grow tired of ponds, mud, polliwogs, toads, snakes, and bugs. They have had their fill of such things. It is time for them to turn their attention to closets, cellars, and attics.

As fate had planned, the boy crept up to the attic for an adventure. He was never actually forbidden to go to the attic but he knew he probably shouldn't go there. "I will simply climb the attic stairs to the top landing and peek," he thought. "What harm can there be in that?"

The attic was full of the usual attic junk—things you see at yard sales. In the back he saw something looking at him over the edge of a big cardboard box. For an instant, it frightened him. A wild beast could be lurking there! But no, whatever it was, it was too still. "Look again," he thought. He peered into the gloom and saw light reflecting off the eyes of a stuffed animal. With one movement he stepped off the top landing and walked slowly across the attic floor, his heart pounding wildly.

"Why, you are a rocking horse," exclaimed the boy. "And you must be for me, or I certainly hope so." He climbed on the back of the horse. "Perfect fit," he said, and patted the coarse mane of real horse hair. "I'll ride you forever," he said. "We'll fly past the moon and travel beyond the stars. There's nothing we can't do and no place we can't go."

How true, thought the rocking horse, more than you can even imagine. But the time was not yet right and first she would have to gain the boy's trust.

Midway Library

That night the boy lay in bed and thought about the rocking horse. "How can I find out if it is for me without having to explain how I know about it?" He had no ready answer and he knew that, without permission, he had better stay out of the attic or he could lose the rocking horse forever. Quite a dilemma, and typically for a boy of his age with such a problem on his hands, he fell asleep.

In his sleep he dreamed. The moon shone through his window as bright as day, and there in his room stood the rocking horse. The horse was alive and she was trying to tell him something. He walked closer to her, trying to understand.

He saw a large tear well up in the corner of her glass eye. As the tear fell his eyes followed it and then he was falling with it. Both he and the tear were in a sky of tears and light and rocking horses.

He woke with a start so sudden that it threw him out of bed onto his feet. He stood there trying to catch his breath. The rocking horse wanted something of him, but what was he supposed to do? It didn't make any sense.

All that day, as the boy did his chores, he walked around as if the air were stuffed with cotton. The attic and the mystery it held loomed over him and he could barely contain himself from running up there.

The next night he dreamed of the rocking horse again. This time he rode on her back and they flew in the air. Somehow he knew the rocking horse was a her.

They flew high over the farm. From a bird's eye view he saw the barn, the house, the pond, even the old antique truck. Everything below looked like a toy. Although it was his home, it seemed strange and unfamiliar to him, as if he didn't belong there any more.

"There is something that I am here to do," said the rocking horse.

"What is it?" asked the boy, but before she could answer a dark storm surrounded them. Giant shapes moved and howled in the lightning and wind. In fear, the boy pulled back and fell off of the rocking horse into the blackness.

Each night thereafter, he dreamed they flew toward a wall of dark clouds where lightning flashed, thunder pounded, and the giant shapes moved. He was terrified and yet together they flew on. The rocking horse was trying to tell him something but he could not understand. The wind roared in fury. Terrified, he again let go of the rocking horse and fell into the blackness until he awoke.

Each day he felt the strength going out of him. What was wrong? He worried. Why the strange dreams? He wanted to tell his parents. He wanted to run upstairs to the attic and see if the rocking horse really could talk. But he could do neither. He had to carry it alone.

"You look positively ragged," his mother said one morning. "Let me feel your forehead." She felt his forehead and, putting on that very concerned face she sometimes had, she went to the medicine cabinet and got out the thermometer. "Oh my, my. One hundred and two point five. It's aspirin and bed for you, young man." The boy was relieved. By getting sick he didn't have to deal with anything any more,
or so he thought.

But the fever grew higher. For two days he sweated and froze and dreamed. A clap of thunder awakened him with a start. The boy looked across his room to where the rocking horse always was but she was not there. "I am dreaming," he thought. He called softly, "Rocking horse, where are you?" He went to the window. There she was, floating in the air a few feet from him. "Hurry and climb on my back," she said. "We have little time."

As before, the wall of black clouds loomed high over them. The lightning flashed and the thunder pounded. Rain hit the boy in the face. He tasted the drops in his mouth. He was getting soaked from the rain. With a shock he realized that he was awake. He asked, "Rocking horse, is this real?"

"Yes," she answered. "But only as real as everything else."

The world they were in was stranger than anything he had ever seen. "We must go on and fly into the storm," said the rocking horse. "This time you must not let go."

"But why is this happening?" he asked.

"Because you are very sick. Beyond the storm you are well. I have waited for so long just to take you there, but the giants are in our way. They want to scare you so that you will not go and be well."

"But this is a fairy tale," said the boy.

"What isn't?" answered the rocking horse. "I am here to fly you through the storm. All the other times have been practice, or if you like, pretend, but this time is real, this time is serious. This time you must not let go."

"I won't," said the boy.

"Then hold tightly to my neck and close your eyes," said the rocking horse. "Do not open them and do not let go."

The boy gripped the rocking horse's neck for all he was worth. He buried his face in her mane. Into the lightning and wind they flew. The giants were there waiting. They roared and howled and gnashed their terrible teeth. Their eyes were lightning. The boy was terrified but he trusted the rocking horse. He trusted her like nothing before.

The next morning he awoke in his bed. The fever was gone. The hazy sun fell into his room and he saw the rocking horse in the spot where she always appeared in his dreams. Ah yes, he thought, we are beyond the storm. But this wasn't a dream—or was it? Everything was quiet. He ached as if a truck had run him down. His mother and father were standing next to the rocking horse. His father spoke. "You kept calling out for a rocking horse and we thought that if it helped we would give it to you early and not make you wait until Christmas."

"But Dad," said the boy weakly. "I disobeyed you and mom. I snuck into the attic weeks ago and saw it. I'm sorry."

"Well, it wasn't such a terrible thing you did," answered his father. "And besides your fever broke minutes after we brought her down here."

"You called the rocking horse a her, Dad. So do I," said the boy.

"She must be your guardian angel," said his father.

"I will call her Angel," said the boy, and fell into a deep, peaceful sleep.

To my children,
The most magical of beings,
Zebulon,
Benjamin,
Arden,
Jessie,
and Big Ben,
whom I adopted in my heart.

Text and illustrations copyright © 2000 by Mercer Mayer
All rights reserved
Marshall Cavendish, 99 White Plains Road, Tarrytown, NY 10591

Library of Congress Cataloging-in-Publication Data
Mayer, Mercer, date
The rocking horse angel / by Mercer Mayer.
p. cm.   Summary: The special rocking horse that his parents buy for him helps a young boy through a dangerous illness.
ISBN 0-7614-5072-6
[1. Rocking horses—Fiction. 2. Sick—Fiction.] I.Title.
PZ7.M462   Ro   2000   E—dc21   00-024305

The illustrations were created in Adobe Photoshop, ElectricImage, FormZ, Bryce, Painter, Adobe Illustrator, and Tree Professional.
Printed in Italy
First Edition

1 3 5 6 4 2